P9-CQG-832

Aaron's Hair

ROBERT MUNSCH

illustrated by

Alan & Lea
DANIEL

SCHOLASTIC CANADA LTD.
New York Toronto London Auckland Sydney
Mexico City New Delhi Hong Kong Buenos Aires

The paintings for this book were created in watercolour on Crescent illustration board.

This book was designed in QuarkXPress, with type set in 18 point Caxton Light.

Scholastic Canada Ltd.
604 King Street West, Toronto, Ontario M5V 1E1, Canada

Scholastic Inc.
557 Broadway, New York, NY 10012, USA

Scholastic Australia Pty Limited
PO Box 579, Gosford, NSW 2250, Australia

Scholastic New Zealand Limited
Private Bag 94407, Botany, Manukau 2163, New Zealand

Scholastic Children's Books
Euston House, 24 Eversholt Street,
London NW1 1DB, UK

Munsch, Robert N., 1945-
Aaron's hair

ISBN 0-439-98716-4

I. Daniel, Alan, 1939- . II. Daniel, Lea. III. Title
PS8576.U575A73 2000   jC813'.54   C00-930505-X
PZ7.M86Aa 2000

ISBN-10 0-439-98716-4 / ISBN-13 978-0-439-98716-5

16 15 14   Printed in Singapore   09 10 11

Aaron wanted to look just like his daddy.
So he let his hair get long . . . only then
he started to have problems.

1

If he combed his hair up, his hair flipped down.

If he combed his hair down, his hair flipped up.

If he combed his hair over, his hair flipped under.

If he combed his hair under, his hair flipped over.

One day, while Aaron was combing his hair, he got so mad that he yelled,

"HAIR! I HATE YOU!"

2

That hurt the hair's feelings.
It jumped off Aaron's head and
ran out of the bathroom.

When Aaron came downstairs,
his mother said, "Aaron, you're bald!
What happened?"

"My hair ran away," said Aaron.
"I got mad at it, and it ran away."

"This is terrible!" said his mother. "Go catch it."

So Aaron ran out the door, and his mother went to pick up the baby. She noticed that the baby had a lot of hair.

"Aaron!" she yelled. "I found your hair!"

But when Aaron ran back inside, the hair jumped over
his head and ran out the door and down the street.

So Aaron chased it down the street.
After a while, he came to a lady who was
yelling and screaming,

"HELP! HELP!
HELP! HELP!"

"What's the matter?"
asked Aaron.

"Look at my tummy," said the lady. "This hair came running down the street and now it is growing on my tummy!"

"It does look a little strange," said Aaron.

"MAKE IT GO AWAY!" said the lady.

"Just tell it to get off," said Aaron.
"Tell it you don't like it."

The lady yelled,

"HAIR! I HATE YOU!"

The hair jumped off the lady and ran down the street, and Aaron ran after it.

Next Aaron came to a man who was running around in circles yelling,

"HELP! HELP! HELP! HELP!"

"What's the matter?" asked Aaron.

"Look at me!" said the man. "This hair
came running down the street, and now it is
growing on my behind!"

"It does look a little strange," said Aaron.

"MAKE IT GO AWAY!"
yelled the man.

"Just tell it to get off," said Aaron.
"Tell it you don't like it."

The man yelled,

"HAIR! I HATE YOU!"

The hair jumped off the man
and ran down the street, and
Aaron ran after it.

Aaron chased it all the way to the middle of downtown, where there was an enormous traffic jam. A policeman was screaming,

"HELP! HELP! HELP! HELP!"

Aaron went to the policeman and said, "That's my hair."

"Your hair!" said the policeman. "This hair came running down the street, ran up my back, and started growing on my face. I can't see a thing. I am supposed to be directing traffic and **EVERYTHING** is all jammed up!"

"Right," said Aaron.
"What a mess! Ten cars,
nine motorcycles,
eight trucks,
seven buses,
six baby carriages,
five skateboards,
four bicycles,
three ambulances,
two fire trucks,
and one train."

19

"And my face!" said the policeman. "This hair is growing on my face!"

"It does look a little strange," said Aaron.

"MAKE IT GO AWAY,"

yelled the policeman.

"Just tell it to get off," said Aaron. "Tell it you don't like it."

So the policeman yelled,

"HAIR! I HATE YOU!"

The hair jumped off the policeman's face and ran into the pile of cars.

"Oh, no!" said Aaron. "Now I'll never find it."

Just then the police chief came up and said,
"What is going on? Everything is all jammed up —
and who put that hair on the statue?"

"Statue?" said Aaron.

"The statue in the fountain," said the police chief.
"The one you kids always mess around with!
Get that hair off the statue!"

So Aaron climbed up the statue and almost caught the hair, but it ran away and Aaron chased it all the way home.

And then he couldn't find it at all.

At dinner Aaron said, "I'm bald forever.
I wish my hair would come back.

I LIKE MY HAIR."

And the hair jumped off the father's head onto
the table, ran over the mashed potatoes, peas,
and chicken, and climbed back onto Aaron's head.

"Fantastic," said Aaron. "Now if I can
just grow a beard, I will look like Daddy."

"No problem,"

said the hair.

This book is dedicated to Aaron Riches, whose pre-school teacher I was in 1980. To Miriam and Leah Riches, the sisters. To Bill and Judy Riches, the mommy and daddy. To downtown Guelph, Ontario, and its fountain with the statue. And to the Guelph Police, who always give me parking tickets and valiantly try to defend the downtown statue from the children of Guelph.

— R.M.